The Untogether

The Untogether

Jeb Loy
Nichols

ALCEMI

Dedication
Thank you Loraine

Acknowledgements
Thanks to those of you who read this book in various
states of unreadiness: Eileen Daly, John Williams, Jerry
DeCicca, Mark Ainly

Thanks too for encouragement: Dodi Nichols, Thayer
Nichols, Peter Nichols, Rob Ryan, Tony Smith

First impression: 2008

© Jeb Loy Nichols, 2008

Published with the financial support of the Welsh Books Council

Editor: Gwen Davies

ISBN: 978-0-9555272-4-1

Printed on acid-free and partly-recycled paper.
Published by Alcemi and printed and bound in Wales by
Y Lolfa Cyf., Talybont, Ceredigion SY24 5AP
e-mail ylolfa@ylolfa.com
website www.alcemi.eu
tel 01970 832 304
fax 832 782

I hold this to be the highest task of a bond between two people: that each should stand guard over the solitude of the other.

Ranier Maria Rilke

1

I was called in the afternoon. What little thoughts I was thinking dribbled out of me and vanished.

It's your father.

My father?

Your father, the nurse told me, has had a heart attack.

I squinted at the window. What I thought was: this is a call that should take place at dusk. A call that should be made and received in the near dark.

An attack?

We have him on a respirator. He's not stable.

Sun came tilting through the window. Birdsong and the smell of something red. The green green leaves on the holly.

Not stable.

I thought: so no change there.

I set out in the early morning, pointed west, the sun behind me, to Wales.

I wondered if I might not make it all the way there.

It was something I often thought.

Accidents, wrong turns, apathy.

I might see something that would divert me, I might end up in some distant region, disoriented, unsure of why I started, of where I was headed.

I didn't trust myself to finish the job.

The car leapt into third; something iridescent fell from the dash and mixed with the rain that puddled on the floor. The puddle hopped towards me and offered pull tabs, candy wrappers, caramel popcorn. I drove in what I hoped was a committed fashion, hugging the top of the speed limit, taking the bypasses, offering no hope for squirrels and stray dogs. The song I sang was: Mercy mercy me, things ain't what they used to be, oh no no.

Just outside of Shrewsbury my mother called. Whole fleets of sugar lice scrabbled behind my eyes. The good stuff, the red sour waggle, was in full effect. My tongue, since midmorning, had been numb. I felt nothing more than movement, inside and out. I slowed down, pulled over. Pushed at empty bags of liquorice allsorts, wine gums, toffees, Flake bars, at cans of Lilt.

She said, what are you eating?

I looked at the clutter on the floor and said, who can eat? At a time like this?

I had, a year ago, tried yoga.

Ate whole bags of candy on the way to class, arrived jittery, spent the hour trying to calm down. At the end of class I was where I should have been at the beginning, relaxed and ready to go.

I wearied through the class wearing a t-shirt that said Who Remembers? I Remember.

The thought of a headstand left me aching and humiliated.

I was inflexible, rigid.

Where had this stiffness, this immobility come from? Why could I not touch my feet? Even the deep cleansing breaths turned into stuttering gasps. The class, I felt, begrudged my presence.

I found it intolerable to be confronted with my own lack of adaptability.

Dank leaves and litter crept around the hospital car park, from one forlorn end to the other, gathering in unswept corners. A man with a broom was pushing everything into a pile.

I threw back one last handful of Jelly Babies, looked across the bleak expanse and sighed. Here we go, I thought.

My own shadow father.

The old man.

In the foyer someone was talking loud to the receptionist. You aren't gonna make me sad here are you? they said. You're not gonna do that are you?

The receptionist did something complicated with a stack of papers. Shuffling was involved, and stapling. The receptionist had nothing further to say.

You wouldn't do that to a rate payer would you? the man asked. A solid citizen. You wouldn't tell him something that would tear him up would you?

His head barely dented the pillow, his speckled neck slack, cheeks dull. I hesitated by the bed while a nurse bent over him, the back of her hand against his forehead. The blanket over his chest barely moved. His eyelids fluttered, the skin around his nose tightened. A sharp rectangle of light found my feet.

You never know, said the nurse.

Know?

It isn't for us to know.

She looked briefly at the ceiling. Her lips parted. People rally, she said. They heave to and motivate.

Things have been known to improve, she said, looking at the door.

I had nothing to say.

Your father, she said, under the circumstances, is a very lucky man.

What he did, she said, was bang a hole clear through his left aorta.

I nodded while she said something extraordinary.

He's a fighter.

Him? I asked, wondering if there was someone else in the room.

Think Henry Cooper, she said. Brian Clough.

My dad? I said.

Prayer, said the nurse, is a possibility. There's always that.

Down the hall, next to the toilets, a nurse was pinning something to the noticeboard. A black and white photo of a dog. Beneath the photo it said QUINCY. And beneath that it said:

LOST – HAVE YOU SEEN THIS DOG? WELL-

TRAINED AND FRIENDLY – PERHAPS HE FOLLOWED YOU HOME – IF YOU'VE SEEN HIM PLEASE CALL 01686 759 947. THANK YOU.

And beneath that, in smaller type, it said:

I've lived with Quincy for seven years and I miss him more than I've ever missed anything in my life. If you see him or find him or have him please, please, please get in touch.

And below that her name, signed quickly in pencil.

Ann.

In a corner shop I filled a basket: milk, crisps, three bottles of sparkling water, bread, some ice cream, biscuits. The cashier had on an oval badge that said Les. He said, can I get you anything else?

There's nothing else I need, Les.

There were people back there, in the darkened rear of the shop, gathered around a table. Conspiring, I assumed. Les's t-shirt said: I'm Staying Out Forever.

In my father's house I roamed into the kitchen and stood in the yellow light. A box of Special K. A glass with ANGLESEY written on it. A painting of bug-eyed children. A necklace made of seed pods. A calendar. Slippers at the back door. A dish towel laid out to dry. A set of cards.

I returned to the living room, turned on the TV and

watched a documentary about drought in east Africa. A starving child looked wide eyed at the camera. A popular actress asked for money. A number scrawled across the bottom of the screen.

A grief-stricken woman was talking. Subtitles flicked on and off beneath her.

She said: once my life moved like water but now it moves like milling corn.

She said she had two children, both now in need of aid, the youngest a daughter named Seraphim.

I was once sent to find my father.

You tell him, my mother said, to get back here right now or there'll be consequences.

Consequences, a word too terrifying to contemplate.

I ran to the place I knew he'd be.

The light was pale, washed out blues and greys that didn't reach the corners. The air was paisley with cigarette smoke and dust. The juke box played 'Papa Was A Rolling Stone'.

I'd done this before.

I crossed the room; he looked at me and tried to smile. When I told him what my mother had said he slumped down and used words like 'bloody hell' and 'dead to rights' and 'inevitable damage'.

He dipped forward and pointed at his pint. The bartender nodded.

I looked at his shoes, his pale fingers, his polished chin. Tears leapt into my eyes.

He had a jacket he let me borrow.

Take it, he said. Pure wool. Hunner percent.

I slipped it on and how little it made me feel.

On the street we ran into Vivienne, who really, my father said, had no business being in that part of town.

Hey stranger, she said to me.

She was splashy and imposing, every separate part of her immense. She waggled her face at me and winked. And then, in what she thought was a whisper, said to my father, we're headed over to Blanche's.

Blanche's, my father said, is definitely not on our schedule.

We stopped in the Co-op on the way home. Chocolates, he said, for your mother.

Cars squished and grinded through the wet streets. The checkout ladies were talking about bus schedules and church duties and the remarkable things their children said. I looked out at the dull night while my father stood beside me and said nothing. He had a look on his face that froze something in my stomach.

He held a box of chocolate-covered cherries.

I had no plan, no hope of getting through the long stroll home.

Can you walk? I asked.

I'll do my best, he said, and looked instantly sad. Like he knew exactly what a shallow promise that was.

May I? asked a nurse.

I motioned to a seat and she did nothing. Stood in the crowded canteen and wavered. Finally, slowly, she sat down. I recognised her. Your dog, I said.

She arranged herself.

I saw your poster.

She nodded and said nothing.

Any luck?

Luck?

Finding Quincy.

Not yet, she said.

I sipped my juice, pulled the top off my yogurt and stared at the blue pulp that had gathered around the edges. Finally, after a few fluttering moments, I said, I'm Lee.

She nodded.

We didn't shake hands.

She looked over my shoulder at the window. Across the grassed courtyard a sign that once said NO BALL GAMES had had an E and a T added to it: NO BALLET GAMES.

Ann, she said.

I asked about Quincy, how old he was, what breed. She said he came from a shelter.

I went, she said, with a friend.

She talked about the bare cages, the smell of disinfectant, the bright lights, the whining, the despair.

What could I do? she asked. What the hell could I do?

Not being one who has ever known what to do I said nothing.

Occasionally he squeaked, a sound that spat dry from the back of his throat. His breathing made not a sound, his eyes rolled behind white lids. I'd seen no other visitors, there weren't any flowers.

I turned on the TV and watched an afternoon movie;

lovely troubled people, all of them intimate and unhappy, embroiled in rich and ornate doings.

When the nurse came back I asked her if she knew Ann. She's new, I said.

Blonde? Big-boned girl?

I shook my head. Red hair, I said. And small. This high.

I floated my hand at my shoulder.

The nurse said, no. Doesn't ring a bell.

I turned back to the TV and saw a woman crying, her mascara puddling, her hands and dress covered in blood.

She called in the morning, immediately apologised, asked what I was doing, if I was available. I'm going out, she said, looking for Quincy.

I'd given her my number. I made a noise that meant yes.

I could use, she said, another pair of eyes. If you want.

I want, I said. Eyes. Sure.

She drove slowly, one hand on the wheel, coffee mug there between her legs. A map spread between us. Large sections of the map had been highlighted. These were where she'd gone last weekend.

This weekend, she said, I'm doing out towards Llanfyllin.

I nodded and she said, what do you think?

Think?

Would a dog go south? Toward the sun, toward the river?

A dog, I said, would go precisely nowhere we'd expect it to.

Like most things, she said.

The streets there were narrower, the houses packed tighter. We drove slowly between second-hand cars and doubled back through gravelled alley ways. All the time with the windows down shouting Quincy!, Quincy!

The shouts of Quincy! punctuated our conversation.

She asked about my father and I said, never knew him well, Quincy! we weren't close, he left home when I was ten, Quincy!

I told her that he was a builder, that he dug basements Quincy!, that he dealt in excavations, that what he did was, he left behind holes.

I didn't tell her: I once put mustard powder in his tobacco. Cut holes in the pockets of his trousers. Super glued shut his teapot. Exchanged his sugar with his salt. Spat in his spaghetti, buttered his sleeping hands.

Ann said, Quincy! in 1979 the Russian space program took three new-born rabbits into orbit and killed them.

In the name of science, she said, Quincy! they kept the mother rabbit behind in Moscow and as they killed the babies they monitored her.

I nodded and she said, each time they killed a bunny, Mummy rabbit would let out a shriek and her body would fill up with adrenaline Quincy!

Science, she said.

I watched two oily boys trying to coax noise from a scooter and wondered what it was she was trying to tell me.

My father frisked beneath sheets; rolling, he turned to his left in a bunched S, then unfolded with a flourish. I looked at the nurse and said, Dad's dancing.

She lifted his wrist, made a note of his pulse.

This Fred Astaire business, I said. Is it expected?

As signs go, she said, it's a good one.

Shows, I suppose, desire.

To be up and at 'em.

Up and at what?

Life, she said.

It sounded a grand thing, wide with chance, as perilous as all outdoors. I noticed that her white shoes were tied with gold laces. A luminous touch. I said, he may be dreaming.

Possibility, she said.

I had no idea of what my father might dream.

I haven't prayed, I said. I can't. Never have.

She nodded and said, I did. I do. Each morning. Before I come on duty.

Thank you, I told her.

I was surprised to realise I meant it.

I called Ann from my father's house. I can't sleep here, I told her. I'm adrift. The windows let in insects, the bed lamp hums.

It's not, I told her, a pleasant house.

The walls were something like pink and grey. Over the sofa was a painting of a naked woman astride a swan. In the corner of the room were a stack of magazines. I grabbed a couple and flicked through them. They were

17

all copies of Excavation Technology Today.

I adjusted the phone and said: now here's a scary story.

I told the one where Dad and I visited an island off the Cornish coast. Our one and only father son fishing trip. A manly weekend away. Enjoy yourselves, my mother had said, packing sandwiches and lemonade. Have fun.

Sounds nice, said Ann.

What we did, I said, was end up humiliated on the front page of the local paper. FATHER AND SON RESCUED BY LOCAL SCHOOLBOY.

Picture a double crate of beer, I told her, a collapsed tent, a dumped and rusty refrigerator, a length of rope, a faulty flashlight, an early tide.

When I entered the room he turned, his hand hovered an inch above the bed. There's been progress, the nurse told me. Your father spoke this morning. Since when, I wondered, does speech count as progress?

I sat and said, hello Dad.

He looked up as if I was miles above him. I waited while he focussed.

Leeeeee?, he said.

The air filled with muted clatter. An amplified voice requested Dr Silver to Paediatrics. The nurse assumed a policing position by the sink. Here I am, I said, next of kin.

His shoulders sloped into what I suspected was a shrug and he said, I had to. List someone.

I told him that I was staying in his house, on the sofa.

18

His head pushed back into the pillow. I watched him squeeze his morphine release. His eyes dilated, he seemed, slightly, to swell. Spittle bubbled at the corners of his mouth. He squinted out the window, I followed his gaze and watched a magpie flap onto the lawn.

He turned to the wall and appeared to sleep.

I should've looked out more, Ann said, pushing a leaflet into a mailbox. Kept him close.

In my experience, I said, best intentions had little to do with safety.

We were distributing leaflets, the same one she put up at the hospital. We'd stapled some to telephone poles, taped them to the bus shelter, put one in the window of the Morningside Cafe.

Our shoulders touched.

It's not your fault.

He was my companion, she said. And I let who knows what happen to him.

I told her how, when I was twelve, my mother and I had gone swimming, in the late summer, the last tired days of August. It was a place we sometimes went, after school or on Saturdays, usually in the hushed afternoon when it was too hot to sit still, a deserted quarry, and on this day we'd gone in too quickly after lunch and gone out further than we should have, we were both laughing and out of shape and before we knew it we were treading water, tired legs churning while we gasped for air, our shoulders and backs cramping. We barely made it back. As we lay sprawled on the rocky shore, both of us fatigued and winded, my mother had turned to me, fixed me with eyes that were younger than they had any right to be, and said, sometimes I forget how easy it is to fuck up.

After dinner we sat on a park bench and listened to sitars on the radio. A family had their dinner spread out on a blanket. A dog lay on its back, a small girl squatted and rubbed its stomach. The family had samosas and a bowl of dahl and some rice and a stack of chapatis. I told Ann that when I was twelve I'd run away from home.

The family dished up their dinner and held up bowls inviting us to join them. We smiled and shook our heads.

I got all the way to Manchester, I said, before a policeman found me hanging around the coach station at three in the morning. He took me back to his house and bought me pizza. Gave me a lecture about drugs, about drink, about the dangers of older, predatory women, about the hollowness of a life without Jesus.

My mum drove through the night to come and get me.

On the drive home Mum didn't talk. Didn't ask me why I'd run away, how I'd got to Manchester, what I'd eaten, anything. She just drove, listened to the radio and smoked. Occasionally reached over and patted my knee. For most of the trip we were on the same highway I'd just hitchhiked. The same services, the same exits, the same signs and fields. But in reverse this time, like time was spinning backwards, like time and my mother were undoing what had been done. As if things, in this way, could be made better, splits healed, holes filled. And the only equipment required were time, silence, a well looked after car, money for petrol and a willing driver.

At the door to my father's room the nurse's eyes were full of tears. I hurried to her, touched her elbow.

She shook her head, looked quickly down the hall and said, I'm sorry. It's nothing.

Nothing?

I looked at my father's room and she said, to do with him.

She fluttered her hands in front of her face. I felt an unexpected wave of relief and she said, I'm sorry.

We stood together for a moment and traded skittish glances. I was sure I should say something.

I said nothing.

Unprofessional, she said. This.

This?

Tired.

I shrugged and said, can I get you something? Water? Some tea?

She turned, I followed her into my father's room. She crossed to the sink, filled a glass, drank it. We finally, after two weeks, introduced ourselves.

I get run down, Rita said. Comes up on me before I know it.

She wiped her eyes and looked lost.

I have a card at home, she said, that my minister gave me. It says: We are confronted with insurmountable opportunities.

I smiled. I waited. I wanted her to know that friendship was a possibility.

Walt Kelly said that, she said. An American.

I nodded.

I need a break, she said. A holiday. Tobago. Trinidad. I have family in Jamaica.

I arranged my face. Travel clarifies, I said.

Helps gain perspective.

I nodded and she said, what it does is it gets you away from where you are.

There was, in Ann, an allegiance to the peripheries of her life that I recognised. The centre remained a mystery.

She told me about the flat she rented.

Hard to find a place, she said, that allows dogs.

Her eyes clouded. I nodded.

She said, they don't let you change anything. The sofa, the bed, the cream walls. Can't change a thing. Very strict. Not for six months. For six months you got to leave everything exactly like it is and learn to love it.

And then?

Then?

After six months.

They have a meeting of the Bankside Residents Group and they decide if you're Bankside material. If you are, you sign a new lease and you can do whatever you want. Course if you're Bankside material you don't want to change anything. So it all stays like it is.

I pushed a plate of biscuits across the table and she said, could be that I'm miswired. Defective in some way. Not plugged in.

Plugged in?

A misconnection. I obsess about things that don't matter.

She talked slowly, methodically, frowning just a bit.

I took a night course, she said, once. Pottery. Couple of years ago. Like you do.

Like some people do.

First project was a bowl. Take a lump of clay, push your fingers into it and off you go.

She picked up a biscuit and said, I got nowhere. Never left the lump stage. Me, a table, seven classmates and a lump of clay. I felt stupid. Told the teacher I feel so stupid.

She shrugged and said, it was ugly and I felt stupid.

She broke the biscuit and said, it seemed to be the way of things.

What Quincy loves, said Ann, is riding shotgun. You know, up front, head out the window, ears flapping in the wind.

Sure.

I'd seen it, a dog leaning out the window, mouth open, muzzling through all that fresh air. I reached down and marked off another street. I leant back to the window and shouted Quincy!

She'd told me to do the shouting.

Your turn, she said as we left the hospital, throwing her handbag over her shoulder, slipping on an enormous pair of sunglasses.

What Quincy likes, she said, is night driving. Night patrol we call it.

On the horizon, somewhere over Llanfair, clouds loomed.

I shouted Quincy! and looked uncertainly at the

coming weather; a single aeroplane crawled between planets.

What Quincy loves, said Ann, is to lean into the dashboard and let the dry heat lift his hair.

He didn't, for two days, say anything. Just slept and squeaked. Every so often a yelp. A short high bark. Rita told me he did it through the night. At eleven o'clock the doctor came in on his rounds and I asked him if this was normal, this squeaking and barking, this talking one day and then the next day nothing. The doctor looked at the chart, at my feet, at the array of medical equipment around us and said, normal isn't a word I use.

I sat in the canteen and watched people come in, sit quietly in the bright lights and hold cups of coffee. The toilets were busy. I spent time looking out the window, watching things that meant nothing to me. Ambulances, wheelchair people, tired doctors, creeped-out bald kids. I wondered about bad plumbing, hippy neighbours, the ugly downhill slant that marked my father's neighbourhood.

That morning Rita had told me: He does not seek God who has not already found him.

I told her my mother used to say that.

All mothers, she said, used to say that.

When I said nothing she said, c'mon, let's chew the fat.

Though she knew I'm a vegetarian.

We talked about growing up miles from where we were, counties away, across hills and rivers, through forests, along miles and miles of roads and motorways.

I never go back, said Rita. Not worth the aggro.
I nodded and said, who can remember the way?
All those exits, those left turns.
Not worth the bother, I said.

My father went south as if he'd caught a bug. Woke in a fever of travelmust and hopped it. I watched him sidle away, his laden car listing to the west. A blue type Ford boat with a reddened rag for a petrol cap.

I developed, at an early age, an inability to use public conveniences that plagues me to this day. I spent days and weeks, a lifetime, inventing stories about my father.

An example: the old man loose in London, a wastrel, dangerous and frail, a hair trigger, grunting into showgirls, wall eyed and wanted, one of those you see, when passing through the West End, hectoring tour guides.

Imagine my disappointment.

I felt sluggish, drawn to sleep and long mornings. I was having dreams in which I gained weight and was involved in public scandal. In one I took up tennis, grew ever fatter and less agile until finally there I was, a vast mass of immobile flesh, piss stained and pathetic, muttering at women, scaring children, flailing at the air with a stringless racket.

Poor me, I sang, poor me. Poor little porker me.

I wanted to hate something. My body, the dull mornings, my father, my mother. All the things that had led me here. To the leaden mess of life.

I thought: I can do without this. His, hers, mine, theirs, the slim and middling things we'd made.

Was this it?

In the morning I threw up a weak soup of ochre-tinted phlegm. It circled the toilet and was gone, another bit of me lost, cast away.

I remembered a woman in a black and white film who said, this misery can't last forever, not even life lasts very long.

The first thing Ann said, after twenty minutes of silent passengering, was, is this a good idea?

Good, I thought, as any.

As any, she said, of yours.

I called my mother in the morning and I told her I had no idea what I was doing. Why I'd come, what I hoped to accomplish. I need goals, I told her. Twelve concrete steps of action.

You're the next of kin, she said. You won the lottery. You're it.

I'm nothing, I said.

You're everything.

What I am is the last one standing.

Then come home, she said. Up to you.

We talked for a moment about her neighbours, her gas boiler, about the way spring used to come fast and hard but now took its time.

It's all off kilter, she said. Something's wrong.

I tried to ask her some small question about my father and she cut me off. Snapped at me. Said, scuze me Mr Gotta Know Everything Right Now, but somethings are just off limits. OK? You know that.

I frowned and she said, OK?

I nodded once and said, sorry.

She sighed deeply and said, there are some things people just don't like to talk about.

Sure.

And for me your father is top of the list.

In fact, she said, making some little conciliatory sound, he's just about the entire list. Between you and me anyway. OK? Understand? Let's just say he's the entire list and leave it at that. How's that? There's only one thing on the list of things your mother doesn't want to talk about and that's your father. OK? You got that?

Yes, I whispered.

In my wallet is a picture of my mother. Taken when she was twenty-two, her feet bare, small hands fisted at her waist. I have the picture because I asked, on my thirteenth birthday, if she had a picture of my father. That's all I want, I said, for a present. A picture. Of the old man.

She didn't say anything, just stood and looked weary. Finally she rooted through a box of photos, found one and gave it to me. That's it, she said, brushing dust off her hands. All yours. Congratulations. Total photographic evidence.

I thumbed the photo and said, this?

She nodded.

My nose twisted and I said, this is it?

She said, take it or leave it.

I placed it on her dresser and stepped back. I was hoping, I suppose, for more.

She smiled and said, weren't we all?

She nodded and pointed to a shadow at the bottom of the picture. That's him, she said.

That's all you got?

She smiled and said, his camera. Wouldn't let me touch it. Insisted he knew best.

She winced at the memory and said, God we were young.

I looked at the photo and frowned.

Said, there's nothing more?

We'd been out walking through once-old buildings that were now new buildings, full of fresh money and small dogs. Behind us prostitutes waggled themselves at passing cars and said things like, Hey there Mr Blue Vauxhall, you wanna get busy tonight?

We headed back to my father's.

He had a lampshade in his hall with all the signs of the zodiac on it. When the light was on you could turn the shade so that your own particular star sign was illuminated. When we arrived it said Cancer.

Ann was telling me that nothing made sense. Like I didn't know that. Like somehow I'd avoided that information. She was talking in tight little sentences that ended unexpectedly. She thought she was telling me something novel.

In my father's house I crept from room to room on tiptoes, making as little contact with the floor as possible. Dust and dead spiders clumped in corners, the windows were streaked and fogged. I'd bought new sheets, a pillow, a blanket for the sofa. The used sheets I folded and returned to the cupboard in the hallway. It smelt of undergrowth, of the funeral ground beneath hedges.

I camped in the living room, heating beans and macaroni on the stove, drinking bottled water. Watching TV. Reading *Excavation Technology Today*.

I said something to Ann about the limited appeal of my father's life.

Lone men, she said, giving the words a heartbreaking lilt.

Like father like son.

You're not him, she said, and I was filled with an unreasonable gratitude.

I slunk into my father's room at the hospital, and sulked. Sucked sugar from my teeth and said, how's tricks?

Tricks, said Rita, are being played daily on backsliders and non-believers.

I heaved into a chair and watched my father's mercurial breathing.

I wished I had some little belief, some dollop of faith.

I watched Rita's skirt drift above her knees. Rain pooled on the car park. Rita stood and threw at me the old chestnut about the Lord working in mysterious ways.

I told her what I'd read that morning in the paper. How a freak sandstorm from the Sahara Desert had dumped 80,000 tonnes of sand onto the ski slopes of western Switzerland. Seemed a rogue bank of Moroccan cloud had travelled north up the Spanish coast, swept west along the Rhone Valley, went east over Lake Geneva. And then rained sand for seven hours.

Gonna be cleaning that mess up for years, I said.

I had hoped that Rita might be impressed.

Sand, I repeated, in the Alps.

In the Lord, Rita said, the unexplained is made evident. I trust in his plan.

Everyday?

All day.

Sand storms?

She had no need to nod. I knew.

Thieves and fanatics? Falling rocks?

Rita stood firm, her faith complete.

Stray bullets? I asked. The objects people throw from windows?

She smiled and I was lost.

I entered my father's room bearing flowers. Four roses wrapped in silver paper. For you, I told Rita.

I pirouetted.

She sighed and said we're not allowed to accept flowers. We're seen with flowers around here and we're finished. They think we've stolen 'em.

Which is what I'd done: saw them in the waiting room, slipped them under my coat and come straight to Rita.

There's so little trust left in the world, I said.

We'll leave 'em here, she said, by your father's bed.

There was a sweet purple glow to Rita's forehead. I liked that. That and her tight-curled short hair. Her pressed uniform too. The way it collided with her hickory black skin. Her name tag that said Margaret. Her gold-laced shoes and white tights.

I liked the the way Rita ducked around the room,

clucking, checking charts, screens, the corners of the bed, the curtains, the lotion dispenser over the sink. What she was doing was keeping everything perfect.

I feigned interest, nodded at Rita's rantings. God's love this and Our Saviour that.

I trotted out my tired stories of Paracelsus, the renaissance doctor. I told her how, in 1527, he assembled the leading Swiss academics of the day with the promise of revealing the greatest medical secret known to western man. And how, on the appointed day, his precious secret turned out to be a bowl of shit. And how, in the face of outrage, he'd held it aloft and yelled, if you will not hear the mysteries of putrefactive fermentation, you are unworthy of the name of physicians!

I hoped to woo Rita away from her unseen god by way of Paracelsus's bowl of steaming shit.

The way of things, I said, is neither right nor perfect but long and dull. A tedious ride through muck and its attending filth.

Decay, I said, is the beginning of all birth! Look to the bottom and see the top!

I knew I held nothing for her.

She smelled of industrial strength disinfectant and my heart danced. Maybe later, I said, we could I don't know. Something like cake and coffee. The two of us.

She straightened and vaudevilled some anger. You and me? she asked.

The two of us?

I nodded and she said, won't happen. Won't happen cause it can't happen. No flowers and no grieving relatives. That's the law. We've attended mandatory seminars about

31

this stuff. Grieving relatives are emotionally vulnerable. Easy targets. So we got to remove and keep clear. Lawsuits, misconduct, reprimands, it's all possible.

I just thought –

Don't try to Luther Vandross me. I know what you were thinking. Your daddy's dying, you're about to be a poor little orphan boy. You got that lost look in your eye. You need some comfort. So you come the crooner with me.

The room's translucent light was suddenly eerie, as if we were knee deep in clear jelly. Something, just on the other side of the door, began to hiss and rattle.

You got uniform fetish written all over you, she told me. I know your kind. I've been there. You like it starched and spotless.

I could hardly pretend otherwise.

I made some feeble protest. Said something about cleanliness and Godliness.

Don't you, she said, talk to me about God.

I took Ann to a movie. Gene Hackman was in it and he went insane. Ended up playing the saxophone in a torn up house. After the film we hailed a taxi. In the taxi neither of us moved. Finally the driver said, c'mon you lot, please, gimme a clue. Where we going?

And I thought: why should you know what I don't?

Ann and I lost ourselves in some distant neighbourhood, near the city limit. I shouted Quincy! and thought of awful things, of pictures I'd once been shown: two naked women on a beach, two bananas, a bottle of rum, a small dog. The heater in Ann's car didn't work, her fingers were turning blue. She was less than pleased, her eyes teared. She was shouting something about hypothermia.

Soup, she said. And blankets. Blankets and a fire. Blankets and soup and a fire and maybe some brandy. That OK?

So let's go back and get warm, I said.

BACK? Go back? NOW? And leave Quincy? Just like that? Leave Quincy here to freeze to death?

She stopped the car while I shouted Quincy!

He may be just around the corner, she said.

She cleared her throat, the air in the car thickened.

I can't just leave him here.

I slurred some damn soliloquy that included, within it, the phrases the healing hands of time, better must come, tomorrow's another day. The great mysteries.

What I wanted was to leave and be somewhere familiar.

Come morning, I said.

Morning?

In the morning, I said, things will be clearer.

The night, I knew, was a dark season, labyrinthine and without end.

The night, I knew, was not to be trusted.

It hardly seemed possible but there she was, in the fresh produce aisle of the Co-op.

Rita, I said.

She looked menacingly at my empty basket and said, dear boy.

There stood at her side a trolley full of frozen pizzas,

TV dinners, Pot Noodles, cans of soup, cat food.

She gave me nothing. A stony individual. Fixed me with her presidential stare and said, do you hold a grudge, boy? Are you a grudge-holding heathen?

I assumed I probably was but could think of none I was currently holding.

Perhaps, I said.

A prevaricator, she said sadly.

I nodded and she said, prevaricating, grudge-holding, and loitering amongst the soft fruits. Hellava life for a young man.

Again I agreed.

Mind yourself, she said, nodding darkly in the direction of the check out tills. Mind that things left unsaid today don't turn into something altogether more poisonous tomorrow.

I nodded.

Take a tip from Rita.

I waited.

Talk boy! she said. Talk!

My father died early the next morning. By the time I got there they'd unplugged and detubed him, wheeled his unliving body away from the bright lights and bustle. What I found was an exited corpus, earthly remains.

Another heart attack, the doctor said. A doozy. Nothing we could do.

I signed papers, made what few arrangements were required. I sat and waited for Rita's shift to start. I paged Ann. Could be that I slept, shut down, all of me wearied and wrecked.

I felt under my arm, next to my ribcage, looking for lumps. I invented symptoms, read the posters that covered the walls. Animals, cars, plants, houses. The lighting turned my skin yellow, the chair hurt my back, the walls were streaked pistachio.

I looked at a poster of a grinning baby and thought: I need to be less well than I am.

I was looking for something terminal. I needed an exit, a way out, I picked up a magazine, felt dizzy, listened mostly to other nurses, to waiting patients, to parents and friends, to the declining whirl and buzz.

2

My mother folded herself into my car and kicked off her loafers, she smelled of rose water and witch hazel. A five hour train journey had brought her from the southern suburbs of London. I lived three streets away from her, in a blistered corner of Croyden.

As I drove slowly through the wet streets to the bed and breakfast I'd booked for her, she said, let's get it over with.

Now?

She did something between a shiver and a shrug.

Show me the worst, she said. Let's see how the other half lived.

I brought her a gin and tonic. She raised it to her nose, inhaled deeply, held it above her head and said, to him and his kind. The strays. To all of them.

I nodded and sipped my water. She gulped her gin and sucked in air.

Music, she said. Put something on. Anything. Soothe me. Something nice. Solace after my travels.

Twenty minutes later I checked her for signs of life. I watched for the steady rise and fall of her turquoise necklace. Her feet were tucked tightly together, her hands formed a rough cushion. I unfolded a blanket and pulled it over her. The day was mild and incomplete; late winter, the evening would be chilly.

An hour later she woke, squinted at me, looked around the room and said, what I am, really, is a little smeary and fucked up.

I smiled and was glad to be with her.

I need new things, she said, pushing herself upright.

Sure, I said. Whatever.

She promised herself Spain, new plates, country drives, more fresh juice, less TV, clothes that meant something. She held up a finger for each new pledge. I scooted forward on my chair and said something about the moon landing.

Apollo 11? she asked. That moon landing?

The very same, I said.

She'd made me drink coffee so I wouldn't miss anything. So I'd be wide awake.

The way the astronauts walked, I said. In their helmets and all that. Their gloves and boots. Like everything was a burden. Like movement was something you had to seriously negotiate.

The eternal and tricky question of gravity.

I nodded and said, one little jump, a stumble, and you're forty feet up in the air. All of a sudden.

Floating, my friend, floating.

Possibly lost forever.

In orbit.

I nodded and said, all so clumsy and unpredictable.

Yet graceful. At the same time. It was a black and grey world back then.

Her father, she said, as it happens, had died in a fire the next day. In the bedsit to which he'd drifted. Collapsed after drinking four bottles of Blue Nun. The Nectar of the Unwashed he used to call it. She had to identify him by counting the cavities in his teeth.

I smiled at her there on my father's sofa, in her misty green suit, remembering that at the wake she had looked sideways at the coffin, held up her glass of red wine and said, one small step for mankind.

It was my mother who told me this: whatever you're thinking, it's probably wrong.

First she said that and then she said: everything you think is right and true and exactly correct.

I was confused. We were going first to a movie and then to a gallery. The movie, shown in a tiny theatre to a handful of people, stuttered slowly. A woman sat on a bed and lost her mind. A man watched. He smoked a cigarette, said very little. The woman finished crying and began to put her clothes on. No, the man said, not yet.

But I'm cold, the woman said.

The man put out his cigarette and said, we're not finished.

Finally, an hour later, the man shot and done away with, my mother leaned to me and said, how else could it have ended?

At the man's funeral the woman stood away from the grave, her hands shoved into her pockets, her face clouded. Free from him, my mother whispered, sure. That was easy. Shoot him. But free from us?

On the way home from wherever we went next, a party or a restaurant, some gathering, we got caught in the rain. It was an evening that had involved dancing and some drinking and lots of moving from one place to the next. When the rain started I ducked into a doorway. My mother didn't. She stood and let everything crash down around her.

Everything was soaked and floated.

I shouted, Mum! Hey!

I wanted her to turn, I wanted her to see my face. I waved once, twice, three times. The night exploded. Lightning whacked across the sky and for a moment everything was pale white and clear. I saw her turn and start to smile but it was too late, the lights went out and the night came black and broken, slamming down between us.

This is a game I played when I was a boy:

1. I'd look out of our windows and pretend that the streets around our house were an ocean.

2. We were a ship, badly damaged.

3. I was the last remaining person on board.

4. The captain, the crew, the other passengers had all fled, abandoning ship, taking the lifeboats with them. They had shouted things like Fear not brave sailors, surely God will

spare us a briny fate!, and Save the women and children first, for they're our bravest and brightest!

5. I diligently searched the entire boat for any remaining deck hands or stowaways. I checked each room and cupboard, under every bed, behind each door. I ruffled curtains and poked sticks behind the cooker. I made sure. I screamed at the top of my lungs, Ahoy there Matey come out, the sea is upon us!

6. Next, using a red metal bucket I'd been given for my birthday, I'd start bailing. Every room and hallway; scoop and run, scoop and run. Full speed through the house to the the front door, onto the street where I'd hurl the water back into the ocean. The work was difficult and I worked hard. Scoop and run, scoop and run. Working myself up into a panic. Water was coming in everywhere, through the portholes, across the gangways. We were losing the battle, we were going down. We were doomed. Still I scooped. Still I ran. Until finally, after hours of heroic struggle, I'd admit the obvious: we were lost, it was over, we were done for.

7. And so I'd prepare myself for death. I said prayers, asked for forgiveness, made my peace with the world. Combed my hair and brushed my teeth. Wrote out my last will and testament and sealed it in a bottle. And then, before laying down on the sofa to meet my fate, in one last burst of pious gall, I'd walk back out to the street, take up a defiant pose, and curse the ocean. My teeth bared, knuckles white, my tiny fist raised in righteous anger.

Damn you murky marauder! You devilish pit of unseen terror! You misbegotten briny beast! Woe betide you, Satan's wet lair, you cursed bringer of misery! Stealer of husbands! Thief of women and children! Evil robber of noble sailors! May you dry up and fade away, you salty home of Beelzebub!

We sucked up oyster sauce and red bits of broccoli. Cashews and pineapple, green beans and garlic. Takeaway boxes crowded the table. For the first time since I'd arrived, the house smelt like a place where a man might, at a stretch and under promise of further nights like this, live a not too desperate life.

Perfect, I said, licking chilli sauce off my fingers.

I spooned noodles and bean sprouts while she said, this is the wonder stuff.

It fled into and through me, waking me, reminding me. I felt ligaments and slabs of muscle loosen.

Hushed things flooded my bloodstream.

Crack a fortune cookie, she said, waving chopsticks.

I powdered a cookie and extracted the slip of paper. You will attend a party where strange customs prevail.

Absolutely! cried my mother. Now you're talking. Now you're talking Pet-speak.

Her name was Pet. As in Carpet she said the night my father left. As in something you walk on.

I passed the bag to her and she crunched a cookie. Life to you is a bold and thrilling adventure.

We got the primo product here, she said, flapping the fortune in my face. You and your old mum, we got the goods.

What we need now, she said, is some gin, some ice, some water, lights out and a movie.

She flipped channel to channel until she found something black and white with subtitles. People out in the farmed country, thin trees that ran straight up. Slow shots that went on and on. We were watching something concerning a farmer and his family. The farmer, a severe old man, a keeper of orchards, had a daughter that named the apples.

Her name was Marie and she wore nothing but faded overalls.

She gave every apple a name. Jean Pierre and René, Christopher and Thérèse, Allison and Jacque. She made up stories about them and watched out for them and fed them and loved them and worried about them and she counted each tree a nation, each branch a city, each twig a family. The orchard was a world and the world was called Golden Delicious. And in the autumn, when the apples ripened and fell, she was inconsolable.

The world, she cried, the entire world.

But they're only apples, said her father.

My whole world! she said.

Silly little ass, her father said.

Don't listen, my mother yelled. Don't let the old bastard get to you.

She'd been filling her glass. One after the other. She didn't stop.

The little girl cycled to a country priest, confided in him and was met with ridicule. She went to her teacher and was told to grow up. At home she had no confederates, no allies. Finally her father went with her out of the house

42

and into the orchard. As they walked between the trees he tapped her lightly on the shoulder with the bowl of his pipe and said, you're like your mother. Like her mother before her. It's in your blood. Silly little asses all.

This guy, my mother said, is a wrong individual.

She held her empty glass above her head, pointed it at me and said, gin me.

I offered coffee and she shook her head. Pet needs rocket fuel, she said.

The world, said the old man, is full of utopians. Chock-a-block. Full to the brim.

His dearest wish was that his wife and daughter might one day be realists. That they might join him in his pragmatism and see the world for exactly what it was. A place where the old are usurped by the young, where the small are beaten down by the mighty, where money is king. Finally he told the girl that he'd sold the orchard, that a market was to be built in its place. This year, he said, is the last year. I'm done forever with apples and hard work and women who act like asses.

He stood alone on the porch and did his best to look careless. The music faltered and the sun set and a cloud of dark birds settled in his trees. The last shot was of the girl picking apples, whispering their names, dropping them into baskets to be taken away.

The candle sputtered out. The gin too had sputtered, replaced by chamomile tea. We sat in the timid night and said little. She had about her the glow of hesitancy.

Finally she asked about him.

His hands, she said. He had the hands of a trickster.

I admitted to not noticing them. I told her: he mostly looked puny. Scared and delicate.

She seemed to be operating on borrowed power. She repositioned herself on the sofa and said, my mind goes haywire when I get tired. Midnight comes and I give up.

I knew this to be less than true; she who never gave up on anything.

Her eyes closed and she said, we just banged into each other. Your dad and me. Banged into each other and thought this is it. Here we are. This is how it is to be together.

I sipped my tea and waited.

She said, he called me Petunia of the Field. Petunia of the Bloody Field. As though that might be the kind of thing I'd like.

Looking at her slacken off to sleep I remembered how once, years ago, we'd been mistaken for lovers. We'd gone out for dinner, the waiter had taken my order and then, turning to my mother, had said, and what for your wife? My mother had smiled, waited until he left and said, that's the kind of thing, right there, that can fuck you up forever.

In his room we found a box of photos and thumbed through them. Most were of women I didn't know, a catalogue of strangers staring at the camera, impatient, waiting for something to happen. A handful of landscapes, a few poorly arranged still lives, a dog in a cart, a packet of breakfast cereal, one nude, a couple of sunsets.

His hobby, my mother said. His spare time.

She held up a shot of a water fountain. It was off centre and overexposed, trees cluttered behind it, leaves clumped around its base.

A master, she said, of the imperfect moment.

I remembered: his subscription to *Amateur Photography Today*, his two cameras, his box of negatives.

I never saw him take a photograph.

We found two pictures of me, an infant sprawled on a plaid rug, smiling in one, crying in the other. There were three photos of my mother, two I recognised, one I'd never seen. In the one I'd never seen she was sleeping, the photo was poorly framed, she was slipping off the bottom, her hair a knotted mess, lipstick smeared, her mascara streaked, nails chipped and chewed. She looked pitiful, the kind of woman you'd step around on the street.

Pet the party girl, she whispered, propping the photo against the table.

I could feel my toes inside my shoes, my elbows inside my shirt. I watched a cat in the back yard methodically lick its paws, its tongue flashing pink.

My mother grunted and said, I guess we were both young, you know, but I was really young. Like I never stopped being twelve. Like I could do whatever I wanted for as long as I wanted with whoever I wanted and none of it would ever be held against me. Like none of it was real.

Consistency, my mother told me, looking vaguely out the car window, takes time and a level of courage to which, believe me, I've so far been denied access. What I do is I tolerate. Daily. I tolerate every last creep in the world.

That's how I spend my days.

I knew how she spent her days. Reading and shopping and being a good neighbour.

And you know what it's got me? she asked. All this tolerating?

I didn't know.

Bleeding gums, she told me. Nocturnal discharges.

I thought I saw Rita on the street. I threw the car into gear.

Rita, she said, dismissing the very idea.

I'd told her all about Rita. About her God and his goodnesses. About her shoe laces.

We were on our way to the funeral home. I shouted Quincy! and slowed for a light.

Never, my mother said, trust anyone who achieves their goals.

We don't want granite, my mother said, OK?

We don't want something that's going to sit there forever and cast a shadow. He wasn't like that. He never got in the way. He was a slim customer, you know.

The funeral director looked grave and said, of course.

Death, my mother said, and its dressings hold no interest for me.

A large painting on the wall said: A Time for all Things.

The funeral director talked at length of green burial sites, tree planting, biodegradable caskets, rose and lily plots, memorial shrubs.

I nodded and watched my mother.

She picked her moment and thumped the desk. Shouted, what we're looking for here, nature boy, is a hole and a sheet! Wrap him and plant him!

A stricken yelp escaped from the funeral director.

Decorum, he pleaded. This is the last chance we have to act with something approaching civility. We can at least have a solemn and dignified end to a life well lived.

Debatable, she said.

I agreed.

About the life well lived part, I mean, she said. More like got through. A life got through without jail time or public disgrace.

A good man, the funeral director said. By all accounts. Businessman and churchgoer.

All accounts? she asked. You've collected all the accounts? You've done that?

Chaos, for my mother, was a strategy.

The funeral director looked confused.

My mother abruptly began to wail. A minutely measured performance. Her eyes grew huge and were wet. She clutched a handkerchief and grieved. The simple thing we want, she said, is to have him in the ground. In as simple a way as possible. Within the law. Respecting whatever codes and regulations are appropriate.

I believe, the funeral director sniffed, that you've confused these offices with those of the local refuse collector. What we do here is design an honourable occasion that befits the deceased; we have no agreement with the town dump.

My mother dabbed at her eyes and said, a simple show, mister, that's all we're after. We're simple people.

No sentimental embroidery. No gnashing of teeth. Let's put the butterflies and string quartet on hold. Nix the preacher. No poems or dancing bears.

Money, she said, is of no importance.

This seemed to mollify the funeral director. Money, he said, is the least of our concerns.

He patted my mother's hand and said, suitability. That's what we're after. A sending off that speaks directly to and of the departed. A meeting of means and needs. A summing up and letting go.

We signed some papers. Made choices and ticked boxes, compromised. Ended with nearly what we wanted.

Ten minutes later the funeral director held my mother's arm at the elbow, called her Dear Petunia and sent us on our way, talking confidentially about denouement, closure, pluck, seemliness, grace, fortitude.

My mother once told me: it's better to be stupid than smart because smart people have to look after themselves while God looks after everyone else.

It seemed, at the time, the most loving thing anyone had ever said to me. The fact of my non-belief made no difference, I knew a good thing when I heard it. I've often wished that that sentence was my name so that when I met someone new and we were introduced, instead of saying Lee, I could say: It's better to be stupid than smart because smart people have to look after themselves while God looks after everyone else.

It would make me happy to say it daily. I would be a better man. The world, due to the constant restating of that sentence, would be a better place.

Her arms flew open and she said, buckle up, mister!

I knew the inflamed tone of voice, the look in her eye.

On the town! she commanded. Shake a leg.

I hesitated. It was midnight. I suggested bed and warm milk. Said, thing is, there's not a lot of town out there. What's there is less than what you might want.

What I want, she said, is the company of unknowns.

Unknowns?

The high street, she said. We could try that.

We could, I suggested, stay home and talk about how things had become the way they were. We could do some excavation.

Over drinks, she said.

I ushered her through to a booth, ordered gin and tonic for her, ginger ale for me. She lipped her glass and ice tinkled. She left behind a red smear. She said, I've seen bad things happen. In places like this.

I nodded. Imagined the worst: my mother sitting slack jawed and dilated, in need of something illegal, watching a young girl, the thinnest parts of her body twitching and popping, dancing on a counter, wearing nothing at all but pink Converse high tops.

The big first step, she said, the slick descent.

I tried not to listen. I let the carbonated fizz needle my nose. The room was nearly empty. Chairs were upside down, balanced on tables, their legs pointing at heaven.

You wanna know, my mother asked, what the

problem is?

I wasn't aware, I said, that there was a problem.

Sure there is. There's always a problem.

An old timer at the bar turned and eyed us. Said, I think I could tell you what the problem is.

I wondered what kind of picture my mother and I made that drunken strangers thought they could talk to us.

My mother said, can you?

Got a pretty good idea.

Fundafuckingmentals, the old timer said.

His face knotted into a grimace, he looked at his watch.

That and golf.

Golf?

Since when, he asked, was everyone spozed to be interested in fucking golf? When did that happen?

He inhaled and said, fundamentals, golf and plastic bags. That's it in a nutshell. That's what the problem is.

Are, I said. Problems are.

The problem, my mother said, The Big Problem, is this.

I waited.

She straightened up and said, where do you go when you don't want to go home?

That's a killer, the old timer said, saluting her genius with his drink. You got it by the balls there. That's one titanic problem.

The jukebox whirled into action. 'Lucille' by Kenny Rogers.

There's always mine, the old timer said. My place. If

you're at a loose end. There's always that.

Now, my mother said, you're just talking ridiculous.

He did something with his face that approximated a smile. Said, you calling me ridiculous?

She left him dangling. My heart pumped. I wondered if things were going to get ugly.

Cause you don't wanna be calling me ridiculous, the old timer said.

I looked around for some small place of well being. A corner in which to rest while my mother drank.

We're all of us in the same boat, my mother said. Don't get excited. You, me, this one here.

She looked my way.

She raised her drink and said, to boats and who's in 'em.

The old timer began singing what he considered to be a sea shanty.

It was then I did an unforgivable thing. As she nuzzled her way through her drink I made a wish. I wished for a different creature altogether. Someone unruffled. Someone grown up and dull and stable and lacklustre.

I glanced at her ruined lipstick. I resisted using the toilet.

Don't look at me that way, she said.

The night left me feeling peeled and rotten, daunted by the possibility that I had yet to live through the worst of it.

Please, she said, looking in my general direction, whatever else you might do tonight and next week and for the rest of your life, don't, right now, look at me that way.

Each time my mother made a decision I backed it without question.

No memorial service, a small one, an afternoon at the crematorium, a wake at the house, a picnic in the park.

Whatever, I said. You knew him.

We met, she said. I was familiar. But know him?

I thought she was overstating the case.

Overstatement I'm allowed, she said. My right. I earned it.

Her latest plan: a green burial, a planted tree, no clergy, no officials, just friends and family.

I thought: is there any phrase that so quickly sucks the air out of a room as friends and family? The circled detritus of one's life. I looked at my mother and knew her to be hoping for the best. An optimist.

And then, she said, home.

I nodded.

Away from death, from Wales, from lost dogs, from drink and its attendant lunacy, from hospitals and nurses, from Ann and Rita and their incalculable needs.

You'll have to talk, my mother said. Read something. Recite a poem. Something. At the whatever it is.

The smile she attempted was lopsided and rummy.

To holes and what fills them, she said.

I smiled and thought of impotent flesh, of liver spots and failing sight, of dull, slow mornings. The next day was Sunday.

Tomorrow, she said, let's be young.

This can't go on, I'd told her once, the summer I was twelve.

Twice, three months apart, she'd been found by the police and returned to me, drunk and raggedy. Found both times on the pebbly banks of the reservoir.

Just wanted, she slurred, to go paddling. To touch water. To get the hell away from things.

In her condition, the police whispered, she wouldn't have lasted long.

It was just, I thought, a matter of time.

I considered myself to be under siege. I wanted things to be as predictable as possible.

This can't continue, I'd told her.

You'll be all right, she told me.

I thought that unlikely.

She held up a spent and blackened match.

Or maybe you'll fuck up and make a mess of things, she said.

I nodded.

In all probability.

There are, she said, worse things.

Mother, I said. Pet.

Mum.

I rattled the bathroom door and said, this was your idea.

It was eleven o'clock. The morning gone, not yet afternoon, the in-between hour.

Don't, she said, make this about me.

Water splashed into the sink. The toilet flushed. A cabinet was opened and closed.

There's nothing in there, I said. I've checked. No aspirin, no cough syrup, no valium, no nothing.

I live in hope, she said.

The door cracked, sandalwood and lavender flew at me.

Ready? I asked.

As ever, she said.

We grouped ourselves in a lopsided circle around a wet hole. It was neither bright nor damp. Something, a winter jay, skipped between branches. A plump woman held a denuded tree, earth was pushed around it. The earth pusher, a grey haired man in his middle years, stood and brushed soil from his suit. He cleared his throat and said, we commit this tree to the living memory of Arthur Gibb. May it grow straight and true and be a constant reminder of the time he spent here among us.

A few scabby leaves lurched from bush to tree to fallen branch. Somewhere, across a field, a crowd cheered a ball game.

I held my mother's hand.

Rita looked at the tree as if it were my father, newly raised from the ground.

The Lord, she said, has a room prepared for Arthur.

Her hair bounced in the slow breeze.

I can look anyone here in the eye and be absolutely sure of that, she said. Arthur, right now, is at home and at peace. With the Lord.

I'm sure of it.

She looked around at our feeble party; a black coat fell just above her gold-laced shoes.

I thought: There's no cure for faith; being here and

making mistakes is a chronic state. And whatever tools we employ to help us cope, create their own problems.

God, Rita said, is everything. Every sparrow falling, every grain of sand. He waits and watches and one day he collects.

Arthur, she said, is in a better place.

I had copied out what I wanted to say. A quote by Martin Buber. I took a piece of paper from my pocket and read:

...imagine two men, whose lives are dominated by appearances, sitting and talking together. Call them Peter and Paul. Let us list the different configurations which are involved. First, there is Peter as he wishes to appear to Paul and Paul as he wishes to appear to Peter. Then there is Peter as he really appears to Paul, that is Paul's image of Peter, which in general does not in the least coincide with what Peter wishes Paul to see; and similarly there is the reverse situation. Further, there is Peter as he appears to himself, and Paul as he appears to himself. Lastly there are the bodily Peter and the bodily Paul, two living beings and six ghostly appearances, which mingle in many ways in the conversations between the two. Where is there room for any genuine inter-human life?

My mother said nothing. I'd thought there might be something, a story, a remembrance. Some small thing she might share with us.

We got nothing.

She stood straight and contained and seemed to listen while the earth pusher talked of regeneration, the seasons, the process of one thing becoming something else. I thought: mist into rain, rain into water, water into ice, ice into a glass of gin and tonic; distant hills, lakes and rivers, reservoirs and pipes, evenings spent listening to my mother talk of simple, unsayable things.

In the car on the way home Ann said, I've been reading about a tribe of Malaysian people called the Tarawac.

They have a custom, Ann said, called Sum Toloc. Translates as "to disorientate". A rite of passage that every tribes person goes through in order to become a fully accepted adult member of society.

I nodded, watched a squirrel catapult off a limb.

During Sum Toloc, Ann said, children of the tribe are taken to a secret location in the rain forest and given new identities. Girls are made to dress and act like boys, boys are transformed into girls. Sportsmen are forced to look after the kitchen while intellects are sent out to bring back food. Black hair is died blonde, light skin painted dark. If one is short they're given stilts, if skinny they're given vast suits made of grass and feathers.

The idea of the ceremony, which lasts one month, is to confuse the dog spirits. The dog spirits work as recruitment officers for the next world, the world of the departed, the unseen. It's thought that if one is able to successfully change one's entire way of being, your look and smell and the way you walk, the dog spirits, who were always on the lookout for young children to take into the next world, will become confused, and, being unable to recognise you, give up. Leaving you free to live a life of safety and security, happy within the nest of the tribe.

I remembered a quote from a book by Emmanuel Bove: *I was quite sure I should never be brave enough to visit happy people.*

To be misunderstood, my mother said, is the most we can hope for in this life.

She opened her handbag, pulled out a tissue and said, to be misunderstood is all that stands between us and that most awful of fates.

She looked straight at me and said: approval.

My mother looked out the window and said, we need to talk.

We? I asked. You and me?

That she refused to look at me I took as a bad sign.

Need to?

Have to.

I slowed as a stray dog zigged across the road. A black dog. Mother of all bad signs.

Is there a problem?

One of many, she said.

Many?

Problems.

Such as.

My mother swallowed air and said, I'm tired. Everyday.

I watched Ann watch my mother.

I'm confused and uneasy.

The skin on my elbows is itchy and irritated.

I have no idea how I got here.

I slowed for a bus that said Town Centre.

I have thoughts I don't recognise.

I have almost no family left, no connection with anyone.

The things I love are no longer being made.

I wanted to tell Ann: walk away. Now. Open the door and jump. Leave us and this place and these people. Escape while you can. Turn and run and don't look back.

The delivery boy's t-shirt had a single word on it: Shitless. He slid his cigarette from one side of his mouth to the other. He had the look of the surf about him, here, in the landlocked centre of Wales.

My mother smiled, handed him some money. Smoke blew casually into the room.

You, she said, poking him gently in the chest, are very definitely out of your element.

Afterwards we poured water, put the kettle on, stacked plates. My mother prepared a drink.

Ann and I waited.

Finally my mother said, always seems to be the wrong time. You know?

I knew.

Wrong day, wrong year, wrong everything.

I nodded.

Don't s'pose it'll make much difference now if I say I'm sorry. But I am. I'm sorry and that's it and maybe I had my reasons and maybe I didn't.

She looked at Ann and said, I was different then. We were. Both of us.

Both?

Lee's dad and me.

She looked at me and her eyes were wet. She said, not that I'm sorry about everything. Some things I can live with.

She took a sip of her drink, tipped the glass forward and said, your father liked a drink.

I was aware of that.

Your father and just about everyone we knew. Finish work down the paper mill and straight away start drinking with his buddies. In the car park. On the bus home. That's what they did. That was our life. The best we could manage. It wasn't like he was a bad man. He was just what a lot of men were, tired and bored and not particularly good at anything.

She hesitated for a minute and then said, at some point he started to drink more and pass out earlier. Come in, crack the seal on a fifth of whiskey, complain about anything and everything and be dead to the world an hour later. Comatose. On the sofa in his underwear.

She took a long sip and said, I was seventeen. Year before I'd been in school, parties every weekend, new boyfriend every month. And then bang, one day I wake up and I got a drunk on the sofa.

She pushed back her hair, sighed and said, how'd that happen?

She looked at us like we might have an answer.

We said nothing.

So I started going out, she said. That's how I dealt with it. Reverted to type. Pet The Party Girl. Pull a blanket over him, turn off the TV, dim the lights and leave. Out into the world. Or at least what little part of the world I had access to. Which meant pubs mostly. Going out for a drink with people I didn't know. Just sitting somewhere in a crowd.

She looked at me and said, what the hell did I know about anything? I mean, at the time I thought big deal. You know? I thought I'm just filling up my evenings. He's asleep, I'm out. Who cares? Who'm I hurting? I was just doing what I had to do to get through the day. I didn't think about it. I didn't think about anything. I just got on with it.

She rattled ice and said, this isn't easy.

She tightened the ligaments in her neck, rotated her chin and said, pretty soon I started staying out all night, getting in at dawn. I'd come in, change into my pyjamas and sleep all day. Your father, if he noticed, never said anything. Never said a word. He'd just wake up on the sofa in the morning with a hangover, roll onto the floor and find me drinking coffee in the kitchen. Like a good wife.

She got up and disappeared down the hall.

Happy days, she said, loud enough for us to hear.

The fridge opened and water ran. I looked at Ann, her eyes were closed. My mother came back into the room and started talking before she reached her chair.

Can I cut to the chase here? Skip some of the gory details?

Your story, I said.

It's just that it gets a little hairy. You know, unseemly.

She put a finger to her temple and turned it like a corkscrew. I don't know, she said, I just kinda went off the deep end there for a minute. Went a little crazy.

Her left hand waved away her own words.

Truth is, she said, I wasn't prepared. For anything. That's the actual fact. For your father, for being married, for being left alone, for living with a drunk, for not being sixteen.

She looked at the thin line where the floor met the wall, sighed and said, I spent a certain amount of time in mud. That's what it felt like. Up to my waste in it. Stuck and sinking and every time I tried to move I got sucked in deeper.

Her eyebrows curved up and her lips tightened. She said, a breakdown I guess you'd call it. That's what they'd call it now. Now they got words for it.

She tapped the floor with her foot, tried to click her fingers but nothing happened. She let out a thin stream of air, a slow leak.

She was talking quietly, barely talking at all.

She said, I don't know who and I don't know how many. I don't know names or places or times or dates. I don't know what they looked like or where they lived or how they met me or what they did.

She took a drink and rolled the glass between her palms.

Finally, she said, I gave up, collapsed. One morning after your father left I closed my eyes and thought: I'm dying. I mean really. I could feel the life ebbing out of my body. I really did. I remember thinking: this is it. This is how it happens. Jesus. And it was such a relief.

She looked down at her feet as if she was counting them. Her face twisted into a knot and I thought: this is the part I don't want to hear.

I was pregnant, she said. That was the stinger. I was pregnant and I didn't know by who. How could I? Coulda been anyone. Anyone except your father. He was the one man I could rule out.

She shook her head, almost smiled and said, there I was: seventeen, ill, married to a drunk, depressed and pregnant with a stranger's child. I was on top of the world. King of the castle.

She slumped back in her seat, her face drained. Said, your father, bless him, tried. For a while. Did what he could. Between bottles of whiskey. Tried to pretend it wasn't the end of the world. Did his best.

She looked for words, didn't find them, shrugged off thirty years, tilted her head to one side and said, who can blame him? I mean, finally. You know, leaving us like he did. When push came to shove. Who wouldn't have? I knew the rules. We all did. I wasn't stupid. I was a lot of things but stupid wasn't one of them. I knew what he was. You know? I'd known him my whole life. Since we were kids. We knew what was what and what was gonna happen. Him and me both. Things were what they were and that was that. Done. What could he do? What choice did he have?

3

I asked Ann: do you know the sharp click, click, the random tock, the dry little sounds that slap one into the next when you play dominoes?

I think she nodded.

I wanted to tell her about the rare nights when, my father home sober, we fully populated the kitchen. The three of us around the table. Black bone squares with white dimpled dots, laddered between us in disjointed patterns.

A game, I said, called Fives. You drew seven dominoes, sorted and arranged them, played a three on a three, a two on a two, a double formed a junction, a double six meant a repeated go.

Later the scores were tallied, added, and at evening's end a winner (my mother, always my mother), was declared.

My mother was a domino whizz. Bang they'd go down on the table! Bang again! Slap, slap! Take that, and that! Crack! A double six, a double two! Fifty-five! Always the right domino at the right time. Who knew how she did it? Some things, she used to tell me, you're born with.

I believed her.

I got no looks, she said. I got bad teeth. I got red hair and weak knees. I got no interest in books or school. I got skin that burns. I got wind. Glasses and no dress sense. A husband I see every once in a while. But one thing I do have.

She held up her hands in triumph.

Is this God given ability to win every game of dominoes I ever played.

Ann and I sat on the step of my father's house.

We said little words, made little noises, listened to insects burrow into dry bark. It was dusk, the deathly hour.

A robin nodded into the earth, pulling at bits of dried leaves and twigs. When Ann moved, it flickered up, arrowing into a sycamore.

It's not, Ann said, in the natural order of things to want less.

Her fingers were inked with wet earth.

Expansion, she said. Connection, adaptation, accumulation.

A bat squeaked in the lamp light, a dusky breeze ambled toward us.

That's what my father used to say, she said. Nothing wrong, he said, with having your cake and eating it too.

Thing was, Ann said, I didn't want any cake, I didn't want to eat anything. What I wanted was nothing. I wanted to be left alone, I wanted to be hungry. I wanted to disappear, to fade away, to not be there. I wanted to be invisible. I wanted out.

She leant back and said, course I didn't know that. Not then. I didn't know anything. I didn't know that for years.

Through the front door I saw a table; on it were two books, an empty cup, some paper, a pencil.

One of the small things we can do, she said, is to do small things. We can do without.

Without?

Without that which by having diminishes us. We acquire, have more, and are less.

She looked at me and I waited.

What happened, I asked, to make you so foreign?

We loaded Ann's things into my car. A small group of Bankside residents gathered to watch. They stood in the mild morning and whispered among themselves. One of them, an elderly woman, approached Ann and said, did you know my Charlie?

Ann shook her head.

Number 14, the woman said. At the end, on the second floor.

She had a look of unbalance about her.

This morning, the woman said, I asked him to leave my house.

Charlie?

She nodded.

I looked at the woman's slippered feet, at her thinning silver hair, there were two dark indents on her nose where her glasses had rested.

I told him, she said, he was no longer welcome, no longer someone I wished to live with. Enough, I told him, is enough.

Ann put down the box she was holding and said, your son?

The woman turned, looked sadly at the assembled residents, and said, they know. He was a man around whom hung a whiff of infamy.

Some of the group nodded. They seemed to know Charlie.

His lacquered beard, the woman said. The appalling way he ate. His teeth.

A worm, someone mumbled.

Worse than a worm, said the woman. Who does a worm hurt? A worm lives honestly, toiling in the earth; my son lives off the gullible elderly, the dumbstruck young.

She turned back to Ann and said, did you know him?

Ann shook her head and the woman said, he spun yarns. Concocted who knows what scenarios.

She stopped then and adjusted her dress. After a moment she said, he kept boxes in his room of old *Radio Times*. Read nothing else. Day and night. Can you imagine? I found them cut up and damp. He may have done terrible things. Unspeakable things.

She looked at me and said, he, my son, had no grace or subtlety. A child of his time. Not mine, I kept thinking. Surely not mine. He was nothing to me. When I ordered him out of the house, he went without a word.

I wanted, she said, to tell someone what I'd done.

I took her to the river. We sat on the sand banks and let

minnows nibble at our toes. We found a rope tied to a sycamore and swung out over the dull green water. We exploded into the river, our feet flapping down into the silky mud.

We talked about how different we were. How separate. How it seemed that only the thinnest parts of us intersected.

That seemed to please her.

She was more delicate than I. Less likely to survive.

But less afraid, I thought, of life.

She was more friendly, more fun to be with. Easier.

While I was more pessimistic. Ready, always, for disaster.

She was, somehow, more realistic. She saw the game for what it was: a heartless, improvised thing.

It even amused her.

While it paralysed me. The thought of minutes, hours, days, weeks, months, years left me dizzied and numb.

I had a desire for her that didn't, often, translate into a physical need.

And then, suddenly, unexpectedly, it would.

It confused me.

I lost confidence in my ability to be in love.

Failed again, I said, sheets in a tangle, pillows on the floor.

Ann smiled and said, takes a while.

I try, I said.

The intricacies, the vague precision. I did what I thought was my best.

Expectations, foolhardy faith, boredom, fatigue.

Maybe, I said, you're out of luck.

Lucky in love, she said, unlucky in sex.

I think I'm not someone that finds it easy to be good at simple things.

Ann said nothing.

I rush. Get antsy. Want answers.

I looked out the window and said, I want everything to be different than it is and I want it different right away. NOW. I want total change.

Total?

All game shows off TV. Ban Christmas and football. Insure the right of working people to own the means of production. I want all cheerleaders and mascots gone. And most music. Big cars. I want more public transportation. I want things to be better than they are. Smarter. And more fun. The list goes on.

I sold my father's furniture. The curtains and magazines and TV I gave to a charity shop. I kept the radio, two bowls, some cutlery, two cups.

I stood thinking things over, weighing up options. As if my life were limitless, without boundaries.

I listened to the radio. I liked the way it filled the room, the way it made everything seem different.

Ann put her few things in the kitchen. Blankets, pots, oven gloves, towels, cushions, a spice rack, a backgammon board. A few boxes of books, some clothes.

Seems paltry, she said. For a grown woman.

Grown? I asked.

Growing, she said.

We bought pails and mops and detergent. We swept and scrubbed, threw out buckets of dark water, opened the windows.

I had a can of white paint and a wind chime.

Problems, I told her.

What is it? she asked.

The hallway, into the kitchen. It's not right.

Not right?

I held up the wind chime and said, I'm thinking a wind chime or a plant.

But you wanted bare walls. You said less is more.

I know.

And now there's a problem?

I looked at my Beginners Guide To Feng Shui and said, we got to slow things down. The chi is whipping through here like a bat out of hell.

Is it?

I nodded. Can't you feel it?

Oh dear.

We got a chi maelstrom. We got chi blowing from one room to the next like some kind of chi racetrack.

My, my, said Ann.

She brushed her hands together, stood and said, we better get some help then.

Thanks.

You get your raincoat and I'll call the neighbours.

I turned and Ann said, you got plenty of canned foods? Signal flares? You know the police emergency number? You got a first aid box?

Morning came and off we went, looking for Quincy.

I thought maybe he'd discovered the timber yard on the southern edge of town. If I was a dog that's where I'd head. The sweet smell, the constant hubbub, the brook, the packed lunches of the workers.

We parked in the shadow of the chimneys and walked west.

Light bubbled on the damp fields. I talked, in what I hoped was an ironic way, about my life. The job I'd left, my mother's strange messages on the answer machine, the neighbours, the situation in which I found myself.

Ann shouted Quincy! and said, when I was six I wanted to be an air hostess.

A stewardess? You?

Ann said, yeah, well. People change Quincy!

I hoped she was right.

I saw something somewhere, she said, an ad in a magazine, a movie or something, and it caught me. Quincy! That was what I wanted to be. An air hostess.

I tossed a pebble and said, noble ambition.

Somehow I got myself an outfit, you know, little hat and badge, Quincy! made it myself out of tin foil and cardboard.

Your dad must have loved that.

Drove him crazy. I used to walk up and down the hallway with a tray, taking orders, giving out drinks.

Ann smiled and said, If his friends came round, I'd get them to be pilots. They'd say things like we've now reached our cruising altitude of thirty thousand feet, or ladies and gentlemen we're now beginning our approach into Singapore International Airport, or please return to your seats as the pilot has turned on the seat belt sign.

I said, Quincy!

And somewhere, Ann said, I got it into my head that stewardesses actually lived up there, that they never came down, that they ate, slept and drank up in the clouds, that their feet never touched the ground, and when he asked me, once, my dad, why I wanted to do that, be an air hostess, why I wanted to live up there, I said, cause you're down here.

She handed me a piece of paper. Something she'd copied from the paper. An interview with John Cassavetes. I held it up and read aloud as we walked.

I've never seen an exploding helicopter. I've never seen anyone go and blow somebody's head off. So why should I make films about them? But I have seen people destroy themselves in the smallest way, I've seen people withdraw, I've seen people hide behind political ideas, behind dope, behind the sexual revolution, behind fascism, behind hypocrisy, and I've done all these things myself. So I understand them. What we're saying is so gentle. It's gentleness. We have problems, terrible problems, but our problems are human problems.

I found Rita in the Terminal Illness Ward, checking a chart. I snaked up behind her, said, good morning.

Without turning she said, still here?

I said, indefinitely.

She moved to the window, pulled open the curtain and said, in your father's house?

I nodded.

She looked out at green budded trees and said, you got plans?

None. I got some savings. Thought maybe the change would do me good.

You never know, she said.

I'm hoping.

My brother, she said, immigrated to Laska.

Laska?

Alaska. Got himself three hundred acres of virgin mountain. Gonna get lost, he said. Go feral.

Sounds nice.

Gonna grow pot in greenhouses more like, she said. That's what they do up there. Cook things in open pits. Walk around naked all week.

In Laska?

They got sun eighteen hours a day all summer.

She shook her head and said, he's a diviner.

A diviner?

Can find water with a stick.

I was impressed.

Is that an actual job? People really do that?

Learn how to find water with a stick, Rita said, and you'll never want for anything.

It's a big world, I said.

Let me tell you, Rita said, how it goes in these rural climes. Rule book well and truly been thrown out the window.

Something, a fly or wasp, banged against the window.

He wanted exile, she said.

I knew the feeling.

From acceptable company, she said. At home with wood lice, with rough lands, with the lowly orders. He

72

wanted to be abandoned.

Always was, she said, a loner.

She nodded at a passing nurse and said, when he left, he made me promise him something.

She turned to me and whispered.

I promised him that I wouldn't die here. Frittering away my time with menial and unnecessary tasks.

She held out her arms and sighed.

This? I asked. Unnecessary?

She nodded. Said, to him this was all a meagre business. The church, the hospital, all of it. Said I was painting the walls while the house collapsed.

She told me that the night he left, he said: I don't want to wake up blank and washed out. Bad back, swollen joints, opinions that don't matter. Never having done the one good thing of which I'm capable.

Sounds admirable, I said. I would've liked him.

People did, she said.

All the long hall was tiled white, each door the palest grey.

My problem, I told her, is I'm unwilling to be bold.

She started to say something, I waved her aside.

I mistake one thing for another, I said. I vacillate.

What I am is —

She looked at me as if I were leaving —

Is piddling.

We went to the Washeteria on Graham Road. A building of the most sublime smells and dimensions. Ann was telling me about signals.

Microwaves, she said, are the ones to watch out for. Microwaves and satellite TV.

She sorted our clothes into distinct piles.

And mobile phones, she said. You gotta make choices.

I'd been eating candy all day. Woke bored, walked to the Co-op and filled a basket with Polos and Maltesers. Yorkie bars and Dairy Milk. Strings of candy beads. Love Hearts. Where blood once pushed and swam through delicate passages, now, blissfully, there was a sugar buzz.

She measured powder into a machine.

Yes to certain signals, she said, no to certain others.

We fed coins into the slotted tops of the washers.

People signals, music signals, plant signals, dog and cat signals can stay. Living signals I can deal with. I can embrace. But I gotta draw the line somewhere. Microwaves and mobile phones. Sorry but. That's the way it is. See ya. Gone.

Our clothes began to mingle in the soapy water.

After a moment Ann said this: in coastal Labrador there's a tribe of Indians that believes death ends in the belly of a whale. They say that when you die the soul leaves the body and is eaten by a whale. And that back in the days when the tribe was small, the whale was small too, but as the tribe grew and populated the entire earth, so too, to accommodate more souls, did the whale.

Our clothes wrestled in the whipped suds.

Can you imagine, she said, the current size of the whale? And the indigestion it must be suffering? All these rotten and unwholesome souls to eat. Choking down filthy man after greasy man, each one more unsavoury

74

than the last.

Assuming, I said, it's kept up with the job and not expired from gastric cancer.

Outside, something small and hellbent, a scooter or a motorcycle, pelted by, its engine hissing. Our machine lurched to a stop.

She selected a drier and grabbed a trolley. We loaded wet clothes into it and wheeled it across the room; it was oddly intimate, as if the lights, the machines, the smells, existed only for us.

And I should have said: these last weeks have been difficult and you've made them easier.

I should have said thank you.

I tried, and failed, to describe her eyes.

They held things unimaginable, the things she daily saw, things I'd forgotten, things that, due to my less subtle and inferior equipment, had failed to register. They were a signal of her betterness, her more complete engagement with the world. I knew that when she looked she saw more, received more.

Blinded, I felt, when away from her.

Ann brought home organic peaches and a potted lily. She stood in the doorway and said, what's new?

Look at this, I said, holding up the local paper. We got something here.

Give me good news, she said.

Some guy, I told her, painted his whole farm blue.

Blue? A farm?

Ann put down the lily, bent over my shoulder.

He had communications, I said.

Ann nodded. Communications.

I read: Weren't God. It's not like that. This isn't blasphemy. I'm not talking to God. This was different. This was like a part of myself. Like I was talking to myself but I was speaking to someone else.

Ann sighed and said, been there.

Took him three years. Started with the house; every floor and wall, every chair and table, every cup and saucer. He painted the closets and the television and the beds and the windows. He painted the doors and the locks. The welcome mat. He bought blue curtains, blue towels, blue bed sheets. Sent away to Shrewsbury for blue carpets. He painted the cooker and the bath and the sink and the toilet. Painted the shaving mirror that hung over the kitchen sink. All the door knobs and latches and window sills and light switches.

Then he painted the barn. The stalls and the roof joists and all the hay bales in the loft and the ladder that got him there. His tractor and his tools. The rough floor and the seed bins. He painted his two outbuildings and every fence pole that bordered his twenty-five acres and the barbed wire that stretched between them. He painted all thirty-two trees that stood on his property. Oaks and elms and birches and two maples. He painted his driveway and his septic tank. When he painted his twenty-seven cows and all his grass and then had two heifers die from being both covered in and consuming lead paint, he decided he'd had enough of cattle. He encouraged blue tits to nest in his blue trees. Poured blue food colouring into his well. Wore blue trousers and blue shirts. The farmer said, now that it's done I feel better. Like I did the right thing and I done a good job.

Did indeed, Ann said. Absolutely.

The power of a determined man, I said.

I looked at Ann and understood almost nothing about her, any inch of her. All of her foreign terrain.

I liked the way she rose early each morning and did yoga. The small airy sounds she made. I liked the unevenness of her, one leg slightly longer, her tilted teeth, one breast smaller than the other. I loved her collarbone, the way she gave away not one tiny bit of herself. Her fierce unjoinableness. Her polished heels, her nimble fingers. What words to describe the liquid moments before sleep? Her steady breath on my shoulder, her hands curled into mine.

I wanted, just once, for her to say I love you.

I loved the crookedness within her that made that impossible.

I looked down at her feet. There were two bright lines across them where the sun had yet to hit. She'd worn the same pair of sandals everyday since she'd moved in and now she was branded. She'd been stamped, the summer had left its mark.

Down the afternoon street we walked, looking for something, a junk store, a bookshop, hardware or antiques, some place to loiter.

Royal Oak Rare Stones and Victoriana? asked Ann. Harris Floor Coverings? Bridgenorth Motor Parts?

We walked by a sign that said: THIS LAND

PROTECTED BY THE HAND OF GOD. We let the day sneak up close and keep us company. I looked across the street at Hassan's Fish And Chips, at the cluster of bikes and scooters that were piled in front of its opened doors, and Ann said, you ever heard of something called a pendulum bear trap?

I shook my head.

Common, once upon a time, in Russia.

A bear trap?

Ingenious, she said.

I wondered if I'd missed something.

We're talking about Russian bear traps now?

First, she said, ignoring me, they'd select a suitable tree. One with two thick branches, one above the other. The bottom branch at least ten feet from the ground, the higher branch four feet above that. And on the bottom branch they put a piece of rotting meat. On the upper branch they tie a pendulum.

What happens is this. The bear comes along, smells the bait, climbs the tree, makes its way along the lower branch only to be stopped by the pendulum. He pats it out of his way. It swings out and back, hitting him. This annoys him so he hits it harder. The rock swings further and returns harder. This annoys him even more. He hits it as hard as he can, causing it to swing high and wide and deliver him a such a blow that it knocks him off the branch. Thus –

She drew a slash through the air –

Causing him to fall and break his neck.

I tried to keep the fear out of my eyes when I looked at her.

The best trap, she said, is the Malaysian monkey trap.

The best trap? I asked. There's a best trap?

Consists of a single hole, she said. Some sugar, some rice.

Malaysian monkeys, now? You're telling me about Malaysian monkeys?

Cut a hole in a coconut, she said, hollow it out and leave it hanging in a tree. Fill it with a mush of rice and sugar. The monkey comes along, reaches inside and grabs the bait. What could be easier? Soon as the monkey grasps the food and makes a fist, he can't get it back outside the hole. Not without dropping the food. Which he won't do. So he's trapped. You just come along and snatch him. Presto!

What, I asked, are you telling me here?

I'm just talking, she said.

You saying that each of us, in our own way, has our hand in the coconut? You telling me to be careful? You trying to scare me?

One more, she said.

One more?

A tiger trap, she said. From India.

I wanted, like the people I'd seen in films, to say something funny, to be supple, to be offhand. I wanted to say: enough of the trap talk!

You coat fallen leaves, she said, with either resin or birdlime, some kind of sticky stuff, and then spread them out over the ground. Along comes Mr Tiger, steps on a sticky leaf and tries to wipe it off. Gets it stuck first to his foot and then to his knee. Then his other foot picks up another leaf and he tries to dislodge that one. He crashes about, dancing, trying to rid himself of the leaves. All the time picking up more. Finally he rolls in the leaves, desperately trying to clean them off. And in this state of heightened agitation he's easily set upon and killed.

While dancing, I said. In sticky leaves.

That's the most awful thing I've ever heard.

I'm just saying, she said, that you have to be prudent. Watch out.

For traps?

For traps and all manner of trap-like situations. I'm saying that things can stack up, one on top of the other.

Things, she said, can teeter.

Sure they can.

She gripped my hand and wobbled.

Timber! she shouted.

In Wild Tyme Wholefoods we had rice and seaweed and marinated tofu in our basket. Peppermint tea and honey. Shampoo. Dried apples. Stock cubes. Ann measured out sunflower seeds while I stopped in front of a display of Bach Flower Remedies. A sign said: Thirty-eight plant and flower based remedies that help you manage the emotional demands of everyday life.

I picked up a pamphlet that said: Try The Remedies Most Relevant To You. There was a check list of ailments. I looked down the list, ticking off my own symptoms as I went.

Unexplained fears and worries, nervous and anxious. Tick.

Critical and intolerant of others.

Tick.

Easily discouraged, hesitant and despondent.

Tick.

Live in the past, feel displaced, out of sync.

Tick.

Experience unexplained deep gloom.

Tick.

Are uncertain as to which path in life to take, dissatisfied with current lifestyle.

Tick.

Are inflexible, setting very high standards.

Tick.

Who, asked Ann, was the last one? What was she like?

We were sitting in the back yard, watching my neighbour's dog chase butterflies. We had another half hour before the midges drove us inside.

I didn't want to say.

Ann pushed in closer.

I said: it wasn't a big part of my life.

Big or small, she said. Tell me.

Finally, knowing I had no choice, I said, Lisa.

Lisa?

Her name was Lisa.

Go on.

Five years ago.

Uh-huh.

We met at an office party. She had those big brown eyes, the kind that never close.

Ann smiled. Made with the big mock yawn.

Dull, she drawled. Tell me more. I want details.

She drank wine, I said. Quickly. Stood tall on her toes and whispered in my ear: shoot me. Now. Shoot me or take me away.

I remember being surprised. Me? Mr Office Errand Boy? Who had lost the knack of easy interaction?

Away? I'd asked Lisa, alert only for failure.

Anywhere but here, she'd said. I've been watching you. You haven't said anything to anyone for an hour.

True.

You're either bored or stupid.

The first, I said. I hope.

She did a little dance. Said, you got a car?

I nodded.

Her eyebrows arched. We were suddenly conspirators. Intimates.

We went to a piano bar and a jazz club, talked about Spain, Scotland, bad movies, tennis. We laughed and felt, mostly, lucky.

In her flat there were bowls of pecans and large abstract paintings. We were quickly naked, we raced at each other. She forgot my name, called me Lou.

It was, surprisingly, for the first time in my life, easy. It worked.

I told her: this is all outside my experience.

She slurred the words 'choir boy' at me and gentled me away. Said, everything good and new and worthy is outside our experience.

The last time I saw her I was hopped up on a concoction of my own invention: powered cocoa, chocolate buttons, Nicorette gum, Lucozade. When I told her something absolutely unique and original, she turned to me and said, tell me something I haven't heard.

We were upstairs. Music banged away beneath us. The room rattled, small bottles danced on the dresser. The bottles held red pills, perfume, oils, pale green liquids. A poster on the wall said: Aswad and Special Guests. There was a sphinx up there, several marijuana leaves, a skeleton, a lion. I knew I was doing the wrong thing, I had no business being a nuisance. The night was a mess and there I was, making matters worse.

She lay on the bed.

The music shifted into something high and frantic, I watched light flicker beneath the door.

Something, either a haemorrhaging organ or the last tidal push of fructose, hammered behind my ribs.

She looked at me and smiled.

It was, of course, a disaster. Clumsy, quick, muddled. I apologised while she called a cab.

She laughed, pretended to look at her watch. Said, three whole action-packed minutes.

She fluttered her hand and said, is that what they call a quickie?

I said nothing.

She swept back her hair, collected her things. Snapped shut her purse.

She had nothing for me but contempt.

I couldn't help but agree.

If you didn't want to do it, she asked, why bother? Why waste my time?

I watched her jiggle down the steps and disappear.

In the slow hours before dawn we began to hear noises above the kitchen. Scrapings. Things running overhead. The sharp clicking of claws. And then, at odd intervals, thuds. I imagined the worst, monsters of an unspeakable design. The undead, right there, above my head. Ann sat beside me, stroking my legs, telling me everything was OK. Just squirrels, she said.

I turned on all the lights and the radio; Glen Campbell filled the room.

I heated milk, made hot chocolate.

In the morning Ann pushed a ladder through a trap door in the garage. She looked down at me and said, you wanna see this?

I followed after her, slowly. At a safe distance. Her flashlight pivoted in front of us. I saw shadows, furtive dark shapes.

Rats probably, Ann said.

I spent minutes on my knees, the air thick with wild smells.

There's something more up here than that, I told her.

Like what? she asked. What're we talking? Ghosts maybe? You're telling me spirits?

I said nothing and she sang the theme from *The Twilight Zone*.

I left food out for whatever they were, scraps from my dinner. I left it on paper plates at night and checked it in the morning. Never touched.

Whatever they were they didn't like nut loaf.

Nor broccoli cooked with walnuts and green tomatoes.

Or butternut squash on a bed of field mushrooms and pine nuts.

I noticed, in a corner under the eaves, in the shade of a cherry tree, a hole. No bigger than a fist. I laddered up, poked around, could see nothing.

The next day, over breakfast, two sparrows slammed into the kitchen windows. They fell and lay still, their tiny necks broken.

That evening we found ten dead birds behind the house.

The next day there were twenty more.

Ann called the vet attached to the hospital. He took a bird away, said he'd call us that evening if he found anything.

Again I imagined the worst: bird flu, highly contagious to man, or something more abstract, like *The Birds* in reverse, the inexplicable but inevitable death of every bird on the planet.

He called at six and said, what you got are a bunch of drunks.

Drunks?

On wine, he said. Wine of a sort anyway.

The berries, he said. On your cherry tree.

The berries?

They rot, the juice ferments, the birds gorge on them and, hello? You got a bunch of very drunk birds.

I said nothing.

They got shrivelled livers, he said. Like chronic alcoholics.

We went back into the attic and found ten more, fallen between the roof joists.

In the early evening I dug a hole and buried the birds. Ann put on a CD. I brought out a bowl and we slowly picked the remaining berries from the tree. The night, in that overlit, spangled neighbourhood, was denied stars. Street lamps and security lights threw yellow circles on the grass.

The music, I think, was Brahms.

I picked up the phone and my mother, in a voice varnished with alcohol, said, tell me everything you're thinking.

I managed to say, thinking?

While she hummed Sinatra.

I was in bed, I said.

Sleeping?

Trying.

Even then, doing my best to be annoyed, I liked the sound of her voice.

I said, turn down the music.

She hummed in an off kilter way, something about summer winds.

Mum, I said. Turn. Down. The music.

The music stopped.

There, she said. Sinatra all gone.

She sipped something and seemed happy.

I've been out, she said. The Crown And Castle. Talking.

Talking?

And drinking.

I knew that.

Talked about you.

Me?

And Ann. With all the people. Amongst other things.

What, I asked, are you drinking now?

Coffee. Black.

You won't sleep, I said.

Sleep, she said, wearily. Who wants to sleep?

I could have said me.

Do you think, she asked, that I failed you?

Never.

Was I, were you, able, growing up, to love me? Was I loveable?

Love, I said, is something you learn.

You also, she said, forget.

Love, I thought, should never be talked about. The opposite of love is language.

I'm going back to bed, I told her.

Go, she said. Go and be nice to her.

We planted, in the man who wasn't my father's back garden, four trees; a crab apple, two flowering dogwoods, a weeping birch.

We dug a bed along the east wall and planted clematis and ivy.

We spread towels on the cut grass and lay pinned to the ground by the summer heat.

We stirred honey into peppermint tea.

We bought white plastic chairs and sat in the evenings, our dinners on our laps.

Ann, occasionally, did lazy yoga exercises.

Tried that, I said, creeping into the shadows.

Once upon a time, I whispered, unwilling to discuss my failure.

You don't mind, do you? Ann asked.

I said, of course not.

What she'd said was: do you mind spending our weekends and evenings like this?

Cause I know, she said, that it's basically a lost cause. I'm aware. I mean, the odds aren't good.

We were driving out through the marshes twenty miles from town.

We seemed to yell Quincy! less and less.

It's important to me, she said.

I nodded. A heron lifted its head above the saw grass.

I've thought about it, she said.

I knew her to be the kind of person who thought deeply about most things.

I'm not under any false impression, she said. About my relationship to Quincy.

I eased the car around some road kill. Something tawny and torn up.

She looked out the window, a shadow fell across her hair.

A friend, she said quietly, to whoever feeds them.

I slowed down. The breeze off the marshes was full of things I couldn't name. Things inhuman and treacherous.

But it's a kind of love isn't it?

Better, I supposed, than many I'd seen.

So long as you don't pretend otherwise, she said.

I thought: pretending otherwise was as good a way to pass the time as any other.

I just don't want to stop looking, she said. Not yet.

I mentioned the name of a writer I admired.

Ann murmured recognition.

Died alone? Ann asked. A drunk. That one?

I nodded.

Yes, I knew.

I've not read her, she said.

I steered the car away from the wetlands, away from that lattice of sinkholes, back towards town.

I told Ann: the last book, the one that offered no escape, that seemed too bleak to be trusted, that was my favourite.

The one where the lovers sail home and find the journey intolerable, where everything they might have once said to each other had been drowned and lost.

Ann, I knew, would never read it.

It had once, years ago, meant everything to me.

I heard a story today, Ann said. A lady in the cancer ward.

This was something she liked, to talk about the things she'd overheard at the hospital. She liked the way they came in short bursts, a new fragment each time she passed a bed.

She liked to hear about lives outside her own.

I moved closer, pushed down the sheet. Her back, impossibly delicate, was smeared with freckles.

She was talking, Ann said, about her parents.

I let my hand drift between her shoulder blades.

It was the late Thirties. The war.

I nodded.

Her father, an early volunteer, got shot and killed

defending a French village in Burgundy. Got buried in the town cemetery.

I pushed at the muscles around her neck.

The man's son, she said, back in Britain, was three years old.

Lucky him, I said.

The school children, she said, of the French village, were each given a grave to look after. These men, they were told, are heroes. Martyrs. They died so that we might once again live on free French soil. The least we can do is maintain their graves.

My fingers slid along her backbone.

And then, twenty years later, the man's son visited France for the first time, travelled to the village and sought out his father's grave. He found it in the shadow of the church, the headstone scrubbed, the grass cut. He wondered at the immaculate plots. At the vases of lilies and fresh tulips. He cried a little for someone he never knew, sat by the headstone, sipped from a flask. After a moment, as he stood to leave, a woman entered the churchyard and laid a bouquet of flowers next to the headstone. He frowned, managed a few words of French.

Why, he asked, do you leave flowers? Why here, for this man?

She smiled, recognised an English accent.

It's mine, she said.

Yours?

My grave.

Your grave?

Mine to look after.

But –

We each have one. Some of us have more.

He invited her for tea, for lunch. He did his best with what little French he could remember. She corrected his grammar. And of course they fell in love.

I imagined myself years in the future, alone, in some blank European capital. I saw myself in a cafe, dissolute, a whiskied coffee before me. In my hand an envelope from Ann. In the envelope are two things, a photo and a letter. The photo is of Ann, sitting in a lounge chair on a balcony, overlooking a mountain lake, on her lap a tiny dog with a red ribbon in its hair. She's wearing sunglasses and a yellow summer dress, she's smiling. To the left of the chair is a table, on the table are two glasses.

The letter says: Lee – How often have the words What Happened? been repeated like a mantra, chanted over and over again by confused parents, by friends, by passers-by, by eye witnesses, by lovers? Maybe if things, if you and I and our lives, if everything we ever knew and saw had been different, if only our attraction and our connection and our desire had remained unchanged, maybe then things wouldn't have ended like this. But they weren't and we aren't and they did and now we're finally stuck with what we are: two people who left it too late to wish that we'd been stronger.

We visited the man who wasn't my father's tree.

It had several leaves now, a guard had been placed around its trunk.

We stood in front of it and watched the leaves flutter in the wind.

You won't write this down, will you? she asked. Please.

Of course not, I said.

Leave this alone. Let this just be us.

She said: I've seen the notebooks. I know how you spend your days.

It helps, I said. To put things down. To lay it all out, this and then that and then this.

Writing, she said, kills things.

She turned away from me and took my hand. I followed her down the hill. A dog came sniffing around our feet. A grey head and white tail. Red leather collar. With jewels. A whole bushel of breeds in one dog.

She knelt and stroked its head. It pushed closer to her leg, licked her hand, then darted off, yelping.

A billboard across the field advertised a new campsite.

Camping and Caravan Hook-ups ★ Water and Electricity Available ★ Turn Left at the Lights and Follow the Signs ★ Home Away from Home.

Home away from home, said Ann, sadly, her eyes darkening. As if the notion of two homes, the one before you and the one from whence you came, was a thought too awful to contemplate.

I was momentarily dizzy, I was hungry, it was late afternoon, I was tired. She leant forward and said, what can I do?

I had no idea and told her so.

The day surrendered. We looked back at the field of newly-planted trees. The tiny trunks stood nearly rigid, here and there one bent away from a breeze. Already they looked permanent, a part of things, a world. Light and bugs and pin point dust frisked around them, an ocean of territory was being settled, divided, landed upon, claimed.

I looked at Ann and thought: when will this all go wrong?

I thought again of going back to college. I'd seen an ad for a degree in forestry and woodland management. I wanted, I thought, to spend time with living things older and quieter than myself.

Finally she said, he knew he wasn't your father yet he let you believe he was. He kept his secret even though it meant having you believe he was a lousy father.

I said: I can't talk right now.

A man, Ann said, unwilling to betray your mother.

Nothing was silent, there was no silence.

We sat in the darkened room, two lamps on, two crooked circles of light.

I heard the night wind dip and cut through the tall grass in the garden. The sound formed slippery, indistinct patterns.

I heard the soft confusion of town life, cars and radios, buses, raised voices and slammed doors.

I heard Ann beside me, breathing deeply, her book fallen from her hands.

I heard something outside, small and quick, a furred visitor.

I looked out the window at the overhanging birch

trees, up into a criss-crossed jumble of leaves and small twigs, all splayed and snaked, too many to count, too many to keep separate, a suspended pool of uneven green. I watched them flip and flutter while my eyes slid down, towards bigger branches and forked limbs.

I let my eyes rest on a single, solitary trunk.

Ann jumped in her sleep, opened her eyes and said, I was falling.

In the warm, lightless rain, Ann in a folding chair is soaked through. Her shirt and shorts, her socks, her hair, everything's slick and dark and pasted to her. She told me, I'm gonna go out, sit for awhile, sip my tea in the rain.

The rain?

The rain.

You sure? and into the night she'd stepped.

I'm fine, she'd said.

The rain falls in waves, an unbroken rush of water. Ann doesn't move, lets it rinse down and over her, bubbling across her face, behind her ears, under her collar, lets it pool and collect around her bare feet. Listens to it pit-pat into her tea.

She has no need to be dry.

She opens her mouth, feels the rain on her teeth. She wipes water from her eyes. Mud sloshes up between her toes, she pushes them down deeper. She wonders if her footprints will survive the night, if tomorrow there'll be any trace of her, or if they'll fill with water, slowly give way, crumble and dissolve.

She raises her mug to me and smiles.

To us, she says, blinking into the unfixed sky.

All of it wet and unwieldy, governed by gravity and chance.

To those, she said, who survive their own deaths.

ALCEMI